The Corsair
Chasing the Mermaid

by
DAVIDE MANA

RAVEN'S HEAD
PRESS

NEVER SAY NEVERMORE

NEVER SAY NEVERMORE

Book Editor: Michael Hudson

Cover Art: Anon

ISBN-13: 978-0692663332 • ISBN-10: 0692663339

For my brother, David Dodge and Leslie Charteris

—Davide Mana

THE CORSAIR CHASING THE MERMAID

Davide Mana

PROLOGUE

Cote d'Azur, June 24th 1952

The view from the terrace was beautiful.

On a sunny day it was possible to see all the way to Marseilles, but right now, in the pale June moonlight, the coast looked like a galaxy of distant stars. The lights of La Garde, Toulon and La Seyne were small bright clusters, and the lone houses scattered in the hills as many bright, remote suns.

"Looks like diamonds on black velvet," one of the Ramin girls said, as she walked by on the arm of a vacuous young man. The blonde one, Danielle, Granger remembered, the younger. She was dressed as a coquettish tavern wench, lacy underskirt, leg showing, tight corset. Her beau was a very unlikely admiral. He nodded and mumbled something.

Jacques Granger smirked and shook his head. Old men think of distant stars, he thought, young women think of diamonds. He sighed, and puffed on his Montecristo, and surveyed the crowd.

The idle rich, he mused. The new aristocracy. He chuckled to himself.

In the cool evening breeze, the party was starting to swing. The band played a silly mock-Brazilian rhythm. Professional musicians hired in bulk, like the catering and the service, they looked stiff and awkward in their doublets and wigs. A photographer stalked the floor, his light bulbs going off with soft bangs as he immortalized the costumed dancers. Traffic was heavy in the buffet area, champagne corks popped like a firing squad working overtime. The punters were already grouped up in cliques and tribes, based on age, census, and nationalities. He knew most of them, and could divine the occupation of the rest from the crowd they were hanging with. It was and amusing exercise.

Staking out the finger-food table: young attorney, dressed like a cheap Casanova, slavering at the elbow of a retired British judge in a piratical outfit complete with hook and peg-leg. Nice choice of costume. The judge ignored the lawyer, and was deep in conversation with the 'décolletage' of a young sprite of a girl in Restoration drag. Granger pegged her as a social climber in training.

Behind the judge: overly cheerful American couple in expensive rented costumes, chattering like parakeets as they besieged a faded soprano hiding her yawns behind a fluttering fan. The yank was probably a TV exec or an advertisement shark or some other sort of 'nouveau riche' from the budding entertainment industry, his better half the sort of social butterfly who organizes charity events.

To the left of the Americans: very sleek sort, Italian by the looks, trying to impress with his Scaramouche act the Pirate Queen of red-headed Valerie Ramin. She drummed her finger on the gilded hilt of her rapier, and did not seem so interested.

And then, watching the world going by, Jacques Granger himself, the only man in the party wearing a smoking jacket and a cigar. Overbearing middle-aged boor, fat war profiteer, rich or connected enough to be allowed to ignore the strict costume guidelines on the invitation. Screw Berthold Ramin and his millions, he would not dress up like a clown, not even for a free dinner. If Ramin had been so impressed with 'Against all Flags' that he wanted to do a pirate-themed do, it was his business. Granger stopped a waiter and appropriated his empty silver tray, and used it as a mirror, straightening his black tie.

A movement in the silver surface caused him to turn.

Talk about being out of place. A guy dressed as a stevedore, dirty denim trousers and a canvas jacket, a white pillowcase over his head, was advancing on the dance floor, in long purposeful strides.

There were others like him, moving at the margins of the party.

A band of smugglers?

No. They had guns.

Jacques shouted a warning, but nobody heard him over the 'samba-temperato'.

Then one of the guys fired his pistol in the air. Voices stopped chattering and the samba wound down own like a tired spinning top, first the piano and guitar, then the percussions, the bass, and finally the drum kit, the drummer losing his tempo and stopping mid-beat. Then silence.

The man lowered his gun and pointed it at the crowd.

"Keep calm," he said, "and nobody gets hurt."

Two of his mates came up, both carrying Sten submachines, held casually. One stepped up on the bandstand, and covered the people from there. The second moved to the side, his gun level. Two other hooded men started doing the rounds, carrying canvas bags for the people to drop their jewelry and wallets in.

"What does this mean?" old man Ramin belched. In his high curly wig and lacy cuffs, the jowly face contracted in anger; he looked like an enraged spaniel as he charged down from the patio.

"Who let you in?" he asked.

A trivial spaniel, Granger thought. He held his hands up, one of them still holding the tray.

One of the men pushed the master of the house back, and the old man slipped and fell, sitting down heavily, his mountain of hair askew.

Indignant mumblings rippled through the crowd, but nobody moved, not even to help the old man up.

Three bandits walked up to their boss. One of them was carrying Danielle Ramin over his shoulder, the girl's feet kicking uselessly in the air, her head covered by her upturned skirt, period frilly 'culottes' exposed. The other two were half pushing and half dragging Valerie Ramin. One of them held her by the wrists, but she kept moving, screaming abuse at him. She kicked him in a shin, the pointed, thigh-high boot causing the man to curse and falter. His partner growled something and slapped the girl in the face, hard, and she stopped her protests.

The boss nodded and moved his gun, signaling them to go.

The two bagmen were now standing in front of Granger. He took in their nondescript clothes, the white slips covering their features, the eyes barely visible through the holes.

"Hand over," one of them said, shaking his bag. Jacques dropped the tray in the bag and spread his arms. "I have nothing else," he said. One of the men grabbed his wrists.

His hands were cold and damp as he undid his wristwatch strap.

"Let's move it!" the boss said.

The men retreated, falling back in a rather ordained fashion. One of the Sten-toting guys grabbed a Champers bottle in passing, and slipped it in the big pocket of his denim pants.

"Monsieur Ramin," the man said, "You will hear from us. For the time being, au revoir!"

And as swiftly as they had arrived, they were gone.

Everything was still for five long heartbeats.

Granger lit up a match to revive his cigar.

The party was over as everybody started talking at the same time.

PART ONE

The view from the terrace was standard Cote d' Azur postcard material.

I leaned on the balustrade, arms on the whitewashed concrete, and looked at the narrow valley rolling down to the sea. There was a white strip of road, snaking down the valley. I spotted a small limestone bridge, Romanic or Early Medievel, squared stones and low parados over a small creek. Beyond the bridge, the road disappeared among the trees. There were houses lost in the greenery, small cottages. And the cobalt-blue strip of the Mediterranean in the background, a slow cargo moving on the horizon, en route for Marseilles.

"They came from here," a voice called from my left.

Jacques Granger was climbing the short staircase leading from the Italian-style garden to the terrace. He was huffing. A frown creased his forehead above the bushy eyebrows, a cigar butt smoldered red in the thick of his black beard. He was in a white caftan, looking like a fat eunuch from an Arabian Nights movie. He came to the top and stood with his hand on his side, breathing heavily. During wartime he had been fat, and now that the world was at peace his girth had expanded even more. I turned, my right elbow propped up on the balustrade, and looked at him. Granger was older than me by a decade, and yet his hair and beard were black, while I had been recently compared to a stray cat for my gray-streaked pelt. I suspected Jacques got his youthful, dignified look out of a bottle.

He pulled a long drag from his Montecristo.

"Those cigars will kill you," I said.

"With that beard," he replied, "you remind me of a painting of Ulysses I saw as a kid."

"You were a kid once? Really?"

Granger dismissed it with a gesture, waving his cigar at me. "Unlike you Martin," he said, philosophical, "most of us were not born into adulthood."

We had known each other forever, and still he pronounced my name the French way, 'Martén'. But I'm not fussy about accents, names or nationalities. It's bad for business.

"There were eight of them," he said, drawing a wreath of blue smoke around his head.

"And about fifty of you."

"More or less."

"And nobody stopped them?" I asked.

"None," Granger shook his head. "They were armed."

I gave another look at the scene of the crime. The terrace looked like a fairground in the morning, the relics of the nightly fun scattered around, sad, crumpled, wasted. A deserted bandstand, tables sitting naked against the wall, a few chairs clustered on the patio, like some strange modern sculpture. The breeze dragged a tangle of streamers on the black and white floor, like an animal looking for a place to hide from the sun.

Looming above the terrace, the big house was still, its windows shuttered. There had been no car parked on the front lane. The fountains were still, no water pouring from the amphora of the nereid, no sprinkle issuing from the lips of the stone fish at her feet.

"What am I supposed to do?" I asked.

Granger shrugged, and threw back his head, exhaling a plume of smoke towards the sky.

"The Gendarmerie..." he said. He shrugged again.

"I'm no gumshoe. Jack."

Granger shook his head. "No, it's not that. The girls, you see... there is supposed to be a request, a ransom note, something."

"That's the way it usually goes." I scratched my beard and glanced at him. "Why are you involved?" I asked.

Jacques Granger was no philanthropist.

He shrugged. "I am not exactly involved," he said. "You know, good guys, bad guys. That's nothing to me. I mean, I wish no harm will come to the two girls, but to me this is an investment. A business opportunity, if you will."

"Acting as intermediary?"

"The cops... Ramin is not supposed to pay any ransom. A policy to discourage such acts. The cops are keeping an eye on him..."

"I saw the car outside."

He nodded. "Not only that. They are checking his accounts..."

"I think I see where this is going."

Granger gave a quick look at the big house. "I am ready to advance the money..."

"What's the Ramin guy into? Politics? Import export?"

"A bit of this, a bit of that. Real estate, mostly. He's developing some areas on both the Italian and the Corsican coast. Building hotels, stuff..."

I chuckled. "And you are stepping in."

"I am helping him get his daughters back."

I chuckled. "You are buying his gratitude."

"Favors," he said, pulling out an expensive-looking cigar holder, "are a form of currency that does not know inflation."

I stepped in front of him and stared him in the eye.

"What?" Granger asked, taking a step back. Then he arched his eyebrows. Outrage lit his eyes. "What? Me? Involved in this?"

I gave him a look. "It's not like I don't know you," I said.

"They stole my wristwatch!"

I bit my tongue not to crack up laughing at that. Wristwatch my foot. Then his shoulders fell and he threw the butt of his expensive cigar over the balustrade. "And yes, you know me," he admitted. And I know you. Do you think I'd bring you in, were I otherwise involved in this story?"

I let it hang for a while. There was some kind of bird of prey, flying like a kite over the valley, surfing the updraft. I stared at its T-shape for a minute.

"I'm no gumshoe," I said again.

"But you are someone I can trust."

"You want me to take care of the delivery," I said.

He chomped on his cigar. "When the time comes, yes."

I let the bus go and walked down the white road and past the Romanic bridge. The hillside was silent. Seen from the bridge, the Ramin villa looked even more abandoned and empty. The creek under the bridge was little more than a stream. There were deep tracks by the side of the road, by the bridge. A lorry of some kind. Cigarette butts had been ground in the earth. The kestrel was still hanging in the sky, surveying the valley, the jutting rocks, and the olive trees. I kept walking.

In La Garde I sat on a bench in the square, waiting for the bus to Sanary-sur-Mer. Granger had provided me with a manila envelope. Photos, paper clippings. Always on the ball, the old man.

The news in 'La Provence' was sketchy. The Gendarmerie was keeping a tight lid on the thing, but it was clearly a lost cause. Too many people, most of them not used at taking orders. Rich, connected. Journalists, too. A photographer.

The photographer had his studio in Marseilles, his name and address in clear letters, probably part of the deal for him to provide his shots to the news.

The bus arrived, and I sat in the back, studying the photograph of the two Ramin girls. Twenty-something Valerie, dressed in male garb, three-cornered hat and all. An eye-patch, a sword and a belligerent, unsmiling look completed her pirate costume, her silver buttons sparkling black in the monochrome print. Danielle, barely legal, blonde and cheerful, holding one of those silly mask-on-a-stick, and dressed like a tavern maid or something. There were a few group shots of the party mob too, but there was little to be seen. No pictures of the actual hit.

There were two other photos, these taken from the family album. Danielle in a French twist and a white dress, smiling. Valerie staring at the camera, serious, in a man's shirt and slacks, a mole on her left cheekbone.

In Sanary, I made my way to the fishermen's port, where my old sloop, Le Corsaire was berthed. I stopped by in the gardeners market and got me some tomatoes, an onion, garlic and basil. From the boulangerie nearby I caught me a baguette, and I was set.

I climbed on board and waved hello to the guy sitting on the pier, untangling and cleaning a fishnet. He waved back, then his face was again hidden by the brim of his straw hat.

I set myself to cooking a bite, and for a brief while the Ramin Sisters were not on my mind. The bells were ringing noon as I sat on the deck with my lunch and went through the newspaper clippings again.

Later in the afternoon I went Chez Michelinne, ordered a coffee and used their phone to call the photographer, monsieur Gaspar LaPrince, in Marseiller. A mouse-voiced chick told me her boss was in the dark room, and to call back in half an hour.

I sipped my coffee, ate a biscuit, chatted with the nice woman behind the counter - probably Michelinne herself - then called again. LaPrince was at hand. Yes, he had been taking pictures of the party. Yes, he had many photographs taken during the evening. No, the Gendarmerie had them all. What was my name again?

I hung up.

The kidnappers made their move the next morning.

Seven hundred grand and change, zipped up in a duffel bag, weight a lot less than you may think. Even in Francs. The kidnappers wanted a million and a half in French tender for each of the two girls. The request had been phoned in, and the police had frozen Ramin's assets. Granger had stepped in, and in twenty-four hours, the money was on hand. Nice and smooth.

"This is not money," Granger said, as I picked up the bag. He was strangely pensive.

"No?"

He shook his head. "This is finance, capital." His eyes were two dark slits. "This is the sort of money that bends rules, that deviates the course of governments and suspends laws."

He looked up at me. "I have a bad feeling."

He handed me a map. "The place they picked is in the hills," Granger said. "About thirty kilometers north, in thee direction of Brignoles."

I eyed the map. An X marked the spot. "I'll find it."

Once again, I wondered if my obese friend was in any way involved in the kidnapping. I knew him for a ruthless bastard, and yet this whole scam was a little too complicated for him. And he looked really worried. That made me worried, too.

I placed the bag, blue, anonymous, on the passenger's seat of the beige Deux Chevaux Granger had provided. I glanced at it as I negotiated the dirt roads, getting deeper in the hills.

"You won't deliver the money," Granger had said in a low, angry voice, "until you see the girls, understood?"

"I will do what I can. It's not like they are going to take requests, you know..."

He had given me a grunt, and tapped his jacket pockets for his cigar box. "You see those two girls safely at home, ok?"

"I'll do my best."

"Keep your eyes open," he had said as I started the car.

Now, the front lights showed me a rutted track, a low dry wall on the right, an old vineyard on the left. The smell of lavender hung in the air, and crickets chirped in the darkness. The lights of a farm in the distance could have been a million miles away.

I was alone with the money.

In the glare of my car's headlights, the scene had the dramatic shadows of a German surrealist movie. A guy with a pillowcase over his head searched me while a similarly masked friend of his covered me with a Sten gun, his eyes black irregular holes ripped in the white canvas. A third man was over by the road, checking nobody was coming.

"I'm clean," I said, keeping my hands up.

Pillowcase grunted.

When he was satisfied I was not packing heat, he pushed me forward, roughly. When I turned and looked at him with the most stupid expression I could manage, I saw he had a gun out, a Luger. In his other hand he carried the duffel. He waved the gun and pointed at the trees by the side of the road.

"Listen," I said," I'm just the deliveryman. You got the cash. The girls..."

He came closer and shoved me towards the trees, the muzzle of his gun pressed against my back.

This looked like it was getting unpleasant. I stumbled in the dark for about three or four minutes, the light from my car fading, starlight a poor substitute under the thick canopy of foliage.

Pillowcase walked steadily behind me, keeping me on track. He was familiar with these woods.

Finally, we came to a short slope over another country track, similar to the one I had been following to get to the rendezvous. A Citroën van was parked on the road, the lights masked with duct tape, like we used to do during wartime.

I stumbled down the slope and finally slammed against the corrugated iron side of the truck. Muffled sounds came from the inside. There were other hooded guys there. Somebody grabbed my arms and twisted them back.

In silence, they taped my wrists.

"What the hell...?"

They slapped a span of duct tape on my mouth. Then they dragged me the back of the truck. The load door was opened, the bottom part lowered to form a ramp. I was pushed inside.

I landed on my knees and on my face.

The place was pitch dark and smelled of rust and gasoline.

I tried to stand, but the truck jerked beneath my feet and I fell forward again, this time landing softly on a body that greeted my arrival with a huffing sound.

I tried to roll around and hit a second body.

I got kicked, I moved away. This one was the redhead, I guessed.

The tang of gasoline was overwhelming. Coughing through my gag was impossible. Once again I tried to stand up, and felt extremely stupid. They were gagged, and moaned and mumbled.

The truck moved faster. Voices from outside spoke as the

men pushed the vehicle. Why push it?

Suddenly the floor fell away from under my feet, and the Tube was rolling down a hillside. It jumped and jerked on the irregular ground.

I staggered back, hit the doors with my shoulders as the van jumped over a ditch. The doors slammed open and I fell backward.

I flew for a brief moment, suspended in darkness. Then I landed on my left side. Something cracked somewhere and pain cut my breath off. I tried to stand. I got on my knees and fell to the side, leaning against an olive tree. Behind me there was a crash. The van had continued its short run and slammed into a spur of rock about twenty yards on.

I scrapped my bound wrists against the bark of the tree, trying to get the tape off.

A flash.

As in slow motion, a flare shot down from the top of the hill and hit the wreck of the truck. The crippled Tube exploded in a fireball that blinded me. The hot breath of the flames hit me squarely in the face and I knelt down in the shadows, watching the Ramin girls go up in flames.

My ribs and arm did not hurt anymore.

I limped along the dirt road for about an hour. Finally, a dog started barking and a light went up in a house off the road.

I staggered there and knocked on the door.

A man leaned out of the upstairs window and stared at me.

His questions went over my head.

I was dirty and scratched, my clothes torn. With each breath, a knife stabbed me on the left side. But I was not coughing blood, so it was all right.

"Telephone!" I barked. "Call the police!"

They did not have a phone, but they did have a battered second-hand Ape car.

I gave a short edited version of the disaster. The madame poured me a glass of wine while her husband put his trousers and boots on. The dog licked my hand, wagging its tail.

"You better lay down in the back," the man said.

I crawled on the platform. The dog jumped up at my side, and snuggled close. The engine started with a raucous cough, and we moved. Somewhere along the road, I passed out.

The old man got me to the Gendarmerie post in Brignoles.

The gendarmes woke me up, listened to my story, and put me in the banger. Then they called the only doctor at hand.

I got my ribs bandaged and my left wrist plastered by a country vet.

"Make it fast," the policeman said the doc.

"Were monsieur a horse, it would be faster," the vet grinned.

I tried to laugh, but it hurt too much, so I passed out again.

I always hated funerals in the summertime.

Not that I like very much funerals in general, but overcast skies and rain make for a more suitable atmosphere.

But the day was hot and sunny when they buried what little was left of Valerie and Danielle Ramin. Bird were twittering in the trees on the south side of the cemetery, and grasses grew high along the lanes between the tombs, a scattering of small flowers nodding in the warm sea breeze. More flowers, arranged in wreaths and bunches. A lot of flowers for two dead girls. The color contrasted garishly with the rest of the scene.

I watched from a few yards away, standing in the shadow of a tree, as I had watched the fire. My ribs hurt with every breath, and my wrist itched in its cast.

A small crowd had come in a parade of cars, following the black hearse. People in black, sweating under the sun. A priest, four altar boys, a uniformed cop. Two undertakers, leaning on their spades, smoking hand-rolled cigarettes, waiting to do their job.

Granger looked like a killer whale, black coat over a white shirt. He stood at the back of the Ramins, offering support.

It was the first time I saw the parents. Ramin père was short and round, his face grey, his sparse hair too. He moved as in a daze. By his side, Madame Ramin was tall and thin and straight as a lighting rod, her pale features set in stone. She was clearly the hard one in the family. For all the pain, she was obviously in control.

The coffins were lowered in the ground, the priest did his gig, the spade-men started filling the grave, the crowd started a gauntlet of handshakes with the parents before disbanding.

Granger walked to my thinning slice of shadow. He stood by my side, pulled one of his Montecristo and lit it up. He was silent. I was thinking about his five hundred, gone with Pillowcase and his band. He was too high   class to mention the money right now, but I knew him enough to guess the missing dough was on his mind, too.

"Bad affair," he said finally, without looking at me.

"It was arranged," I said.

He turned and stared. "That's what you told the cops?"

I nodded. "Not that they believed me, or cared."

He grunted, and blew some smoke. "Arranged how?"

"Cars don't blow up like that when they crash.   Lorries neither. The cargo area smelt of gasoline. They used a flare gun. They wanted to kill us."

Granger cursed under his breath.

"Mister Martin?"

I turned, and Madame Ramin's gaze nailed me where I stood.

"Just Martin," I said on reflex.

She kept staring at me, her eyes blue and icy.

"I am sorry," I tried. My voice came out as a croak.

She shook her head, a single snap of her neck, like one of those wind-up toys.

"Find them," she said.

"The police..." I said, but she cut me short.

"I don't care for the police. You find the bastards who killed my daughters."

Granger stepped in, holding her arm and trying to drag her to her car. Her husband was standing there, looking at us, his face a gray oval with black glasses.

"Come," the fat man said, pulling her gently. "I'm sure they will be caught..."

Madame Ramin was immovable as a rock, and she kept staring at me in the eye.

"I'll try," I said.

She nodded, again a single head snap, and finally allowed Granger to pull her to her car.

"I don't want them arrested," she said. "I want them to suffer."

I tried.

The two girls were heavy on my conscience, much more than the missing money. I had been so close and so useless; I was ashamed of myself. I had let them down.

I spent two weeks, while my wrist went back to normal, trying to pick up the scent of the killers. But wherever I looked, I drew a blank.

The truck had been stolen in Marseilles.

The police had no fingerprints and no leads, or if they had, they were not willing to share. I could not blame them.

The papers blared about the killing for about a week. Then a couple of American actors took a break from filming in Rome and made their appearance on the Promenade des Anglais, and the papers had something fresher and happier to report.

I met the photographer, in his Marseilles studio. He was a slick number with a pencil thin mustache, and he had smelled blood in the water. He played it close to his chest. He wanted money in exchange for the photographs. I let it go. As I left the studio, his blonde assistant eyed me, and waved goodbye with her small, well-manicured hand.

And as the days passed, the trail cooled.

I had counted five men, medium build, no significant features. Only Pillowcase had spoken briefly, and his voice was just a voice. According to Granger there had been eight men when they hit the Ramin party. Keeping a secret when there's eight men involved is hard. Something should leak out.

Granger helped, getting in touch with old Maquis confederates, trying to track the weapons, asking the guys to keep an ear to the ground. But his inquiries went nowhere, too.

I met Madame Ramin once, in her parlor. She was cold as ice, distant, detached. I explained my continued failure in tracking the men who had killed her daughters. She took the news with absolute indifference.

In early August, Madame Ramin went back to Paris.

Summer was in full swing along the coast, but as far as my efforts were concerned, nothing moved. And then the summer was gone too and the Cote became a dreary place of lonely palm trees and windswept, deserted promenades. It started raining, the clouds rolled in from the sea.

Autumn.

My wrist back in working order, I took my leave from Granger's, and sailed away. I was looking for a place where I could sleep again without dreams of fireballs erupting in the dark, and dying girls.

PART TWO

I moved east against the wind. The Italian Riviera was even drearier than its French counterpart. Lonesome gravelly beaches, deserted ports, all the boats pulled aground.

I stopped in Menton, and then in Ventimiglia and Diano Marina. In Diano there was a kid flying a kite. It soared, bright red, over the beach.

I don't believe in signs, but I dropped anchor in sight of the new jetty, and spent the night below decks. It was the first night of good sleep in a long while. No balls of flames engulfing trucks, no girls screaming.

In the next days I kept following the coast, and came to the dark gray blot that's Genoa. The plan was to move along, sailing by the Cinque Terre, and then south, to the quiet coast of Tuscany. In Genoa I stopped for a few hours. There's a small bookstore, halfway up to the Principe area, that trades in 'foreign language', (that is, not Italian) books. I've got a deal with the owner. I hand him back the books I've already read, and barter for new ones. A good way to manage the small space that Le Corsair allows, and still have something good to read.

Bruno Campanella was a bookseller before the war. The Regime and then the Nazis had forced him in another kind of business.

"Long time no see," he smirked from behind the counter. He was wearing a tweed hat.

"I've been across the border," I replied, placing a packet of books in front of him. He examined the lot.

"I guessed you would keep the Heyerdahl book," he said.

His prodigious memory had been one of his assets during the war.

He held up one of the books. "There's a new one out," he said.

"It's gonna be a long series if he has to make it to admiral."

He bought back the lot - the Hornblower, the two Asimovs and the Pavese and the stack of Dickson Carrs.

"No Martian Chronicles?" he asked, holding the book up.

"I hated it."

He shook his head.

In the end I got a thing called 'To Catch a Thief', a historical thing set in Bengal, and a collection of ghost stories edited by the Solar Pons guy. Barter closed satisfactorily for the both of us, we spent about one hour talking books, current events and old acquaintances. It was then that "I've got something for you," Bruno said. He opened a drawer and gave me a letter.

"It was left here for you, last month," he said.

I opened it.

A single sheet, in a neat, precise feminine hand.

"Problems?" Bruno asked.

I nodded. "Do you remember Damiano Bricco?"

"Of course I remember," he replied, serious. "Code-name The Miser. Old Communist. He was one of the across-the-border men.

Good at forging documents. Now he lives somewhere near

Imperia."

"Not anymore," I said.

Cypresses like black fingers pointing at the sky, the small village cemetery felt deserted and forlorn. There was the smell of smoke in the air, and the wind was bitter cold. Gravel crunching beneath my soles, it took me about ten minutes to find Damiano's grave. There was a small bunch of white daisies in a tin vase, and one of those sepia-colored pictures, an old photo of my friend, taken before the war.

I crouched down, and placed a hand on the white marble gravestone.

It was cheap, with bas-relief letters and a sepia-tone photo, and a small support for its tin vase. A name, two dates, the sugar-like texture of the stone. Nothing wrong with that: "Save the money for the living," Damiano used to say.

Damiano Bricco had gone while I was in France. My mind was strangely blank - no great memories of moments spent together came to me as I stood there. I knew, rationally, that we had been through a few tight moments, back in the winter of '44, but in that precise moment it was all gone.

I tried desperately to visualize a night, up by Badalucco. The fog, the Germans and the 'Republichini'. That night had seemed to last forever - but it was then, and I was younger, and scared. Now it was only a collection of shadows and ghosts.

I pulled up the collar of my jacket, and walked back to the exit.

Tamara was waiting there for me, a stark charcoal sketch by the side of a forbidding black cypress. She stared at me, serious, with the same expression she used to have as a child. The wind was playing with her black hair. She was wearing a man's overcoat, the army-style cut suggesting the green fabric had been dyed black.

"They told me you where back," she said when I was close enough.

"I got your letter," I said.

She embraced me, and kissed both my cheeks. She smelt of soap and tobacco.

"Sorry I'm late," I whispered.

Tamara gave a brief shrug. "Come," she said. "Let's have something to drink."

She had a bicycle, an old black man's bike, leaning against the outer wall of the cemetery. We walked together back to the village, trading the sort of small talk old time friends use to tighten the bonds, after a long absence.

A gray stone box with a slate roof, on the inside Damiano's old place was dim and crowded with stuff - baskets, wooden boxes filled with empty bottles, books and newspapers stacked at random, glass jars with decrepit labels. Tamara got rid of her black overcoat, lit an old storm lamp, and gestured for me to sit down while she revived the old stove. Bright orange sparks erupted as she fed another faggot into the belly of the thing. She shook her head, her hair brushing her shoulders.

"Coffee?" she asked.

She did not wait for my answer, and shoveled coffee powder into the filter of a six-cups Neapolitan coffee pot. She placed the thing on the stove as I waded through the jumble and reached the table she had pointed at. I moved a pile of books on the floor and sat on the bench beneath a dirty window.

"I tried to reach you," she said, standing with her arms crossed. "When it happened, I mean. But you were sailing somewhere or other."

I nodded. "What happened, exactly?"

She gave a shrug, and turned to check the coffee.

"He was coming home, on his bicycle," she said. "From the seaside."

Damiano had complemented his pension with his paintings, and sketching tourist portraits on the Lungomare.

"A car rammed him from behind, and ran over him."

I cursed.

She picked up the coffee pot and turned it over, allowing for the coffee to drip through. The burnt smell invaded the room, enlivening the stale, dusty air.

Two mismatched cups, a glass jar with sugar, a single coffee-spoon between the two of us. Tamara placed her crumpled pack of Nazionali on the table. Then she looked around, picked a match from the shelf by the stove, and finally sat down.

"They said it was an accident," she said.

She struck the match on the rough surface of the table, and lit a cigarette. "He had been drinking," she said, matter-of-factly.

I poured the coffee.

"He always lived like a stray cat," she said, "and he died like one."

"You're hard."

"I have to be. Is there a more stupid way to die?"

I put some sugar in her coffee. She stopped me on the second spoonful. Her hands were raw, the hands of a working woman.

"Do they know who it was, how it happened?"

A shrug. "Nobody saw anything. Two fishermen found him. They saw the bicycle in the gutter, walked over, and there he was, his neck broken."

She sipped her coffee. "The cops said whoever it was they were going fast. Probably somebody form around here."

"It was down by the coast."

"Yes," she said. "About two kilometers out of Arma."

She meant Arma di Taggia, one of the tourist spots where Damiano used to ply his trade.

"And in broad daylight," she added, shaking her head.

We sat in silence for a few minutes, each one chasing their thoughts.

"If I can help in any way..." I said, finally.

Tamara nodded, stubbing out her fag. "I think there's something you might do for me."

I arched my eyebrows.

"The only good thing he left me is his bicycle," she said. "But the old man left a lot of junk behind," she gave a look around. "As you can see."

"He always was a pack-rat."

"Yeah. He also left a few bills to settle. Quite a few. That, too, was just like him." She gave me a sad smile. "Would you mind going through his stuff, see if there's something that could be sold? You got contacts..."

I nodded. "I do. I'll see what can be made of your father's stuff."

"There's a set of his marinas," she said. "Other paintings, too. And then all the stuff... canvases, easel, paint tubes."

"I can buy you those," I said. "And then I'll find a buyer for your father's paintings. It should not be hard, even if this is not exactly the right season."

Tamara nodded a thank you. She went to pick another match. She lit up, and then she stared at me. Her eyes were green, and crystal clear. She blew the match out.

I stood. It was time to leave. I looked out of the window, the small courtyard veiled by the thick layer of dirt on the glass pane. The place was in shambles. I saw the black bicycle leaning by the gate. Something flickered at the back of my mind.

"Where did you get the bicycle repaired?" I asked her.

She looked at me. "I didn't."

I turned to stare at her.

"Do you have a place to sleep?" she asked.

"Le Corsair's moored in Santo Stefano," I said.

She chuckled. "I mean a place where you can actually stretch your legs. It will take a few days, going through the old man's stuff."

I sat back, slowly. "You got any idea?"

"You could stay here for the duration."

I looked around the overcrowded room.

"You sure you got the space?"

She grinned. "I've got a very big bed," she said.

In the early morning light, I started bringing a semblance of order to the chaos that was my dead friend's studio. This was the room in which Damiano Bricco had spent most of his time when he was home. The wooden floor was stained with splashes of color, and the walls were covered in shelves, holding a variety of jars, bottles and boxes. A pile of folders and portfolios was stacked behind the door, together with a small wooden box smeared with colored chalk fingerprints.

"That stuff was on my bed," Tamara nodded. She placed a steaming tin mug on the small table, between brushes, dried up pots of paint and stained jars from which solvents had long evaporated. I stood there, arms wrapped around my chest to keep warm, looking around.

"Told you it would take time," she winked.

I sighed, took a sip of the long coffee. Probably made recycling the powder of yesterday's espresso. I watched her as she left the room, wrapped in an old shawl. Money was tight; winter was closing in.

I was halfway through my morning coffee when she took off on her black bicycle. I set to work, starting on the paintings.

Damiano always had a good hand. He was a natural, at ease with a variety of mediums and subjects: watercolors, tempera, charcoal, landscapes, portraits, still lives; he could do everything. Damiano's paintings had it all, the bright colors, the poetic flair, a certain quality of the light that sets great artists apart from the rabble. I cleared a table and started stacking the paintings based on medium, dimensions, variety and price range.

I knew a few galleries, along the Cote d'Azur, that would take some of these and pay a good price. The Northern shore of the Mediterranean is uniform enough: you can sell in Provence a vista of the Tuscan Gran Sasso or the Ligurian Capra Zoppa in Finale Ligure, and actually talk the punters, mostly Brits and Americans, into believing it's Les Alpilles.

The watercolors would probably go faster. But there were a few still lives, vaguely Renaissance in style, that could fetch a nice figure, in the right shop window.

In the early afternoon, Tamara was back with a basket full of groceries. I did a quick survey of the art materials. Two easels in good condition. I did not need those, and I knew a seller of art supplies who would take them, after a quick cleaning and polishing. I found half a bottle of wax on a shelf, and some very fine sandpaper in a drawer, and decided to spend the rest of the evening working on the wooden contraptions. I scraped the frames clean and waxed the wood while Tamara cooked dinner on the stove. We talked during our meal and then, the night being cold and dark, we retreated to her room.

Tamara huddled closer. I could smell the soap on her skin in the dark, the stale tobacco on her breath, and the warmth of her body.

"What are you thinking about?" she whispered.

"You should be asleep," I said.

"I can't," she said, pulling closer. "I hear the gears in your brain, turning and clicking like machinery. What are you thinking about?"

I sighed, and moved to shift the rough wool blanket, so that it would seal us off the chill of the bedroom.

"It's strange," I said finally.

"What?"

"A car slamming in a bicycle hard enough to push it off the road and kill the cyclist, and yet leaving the bicycle undamaged."

She moved a little, a sudden stiffness in her limbs. "What do you mean?"

"Nothing," I said. "Only, it's strange, that's all."

She was silent for a long moment; I thought she had fallen asleep. Then she sighed, her warm breath on my cheek, and she turned, facing away from me. A few moments later she was snoring.

I kept staring at the darkness above us.

The next day I spent the morning sorting out the paintings. Then after lunch I picked up two large portfolios that I had slipped between the leg of the working table and the wall, and checked the contents.

White fabriano paper, with charcoal sketches, mostly portraits and group scenes. Between April and September,

Damiano had been moving up and down the Riviera coast, hitting all the tourist spots.

A competent artist can get by throughout the summer, along the Cote and the Riviera. There is a way, you see. You find a nice scenic spot along the promenade, and you select a nice table in the large outer area of the best seaside cafe. You order a cappuccino and a croissant, or maybe a slice of focaccia. Nothing fancy, nothing too expensive. You must not overdo it. While you wait for your order, you set up your stuff, the pencils and charcoals, the block, and all the rest. As soon as you are served your breakfast, you start sketching. With ease, but fast enough to complete one or two pieces while your cappuccino lasts. The trick, here, is to look the part. You must strike the punters as an 'artiste': white trousers, a colorful but not-too-garish shirt, and a pair of espadrilles at your feet. Be kind and reserved, but ready to strike a conversation. Soon a small crowd of beach-goers and tourists will gather around, watching you at work. It is a good arrangement, one the owner of the cafe can understand and appreciate without effort. The crowd means more clients for the venue, and so they'll be happy to offer you your simple breakfast. If you are really good they might even ask you to come back. In the meantime, a few people will ask you to do their portrait. They will tip you for it. Don't put up a price sign. Show some class; don't confirm the obvious suspicion you are in it for the money. Let things happen. Help them happen by being cheerful and easy. Then you can move to a brasserie for lunch, and then relocate to a bar further along the promenade for the afternoon. You have to be good enough to do it, fast and engaging, and show a modicum of competence in your artwork.

And Damiano was quite good. He was one of the best. Good enough to make a living out of it, six months a year. He would sit there, his shirtsleeves rolled up, a cigarette dangling nonchalantly from his lips, fingers brushing the paper as he captured a face, an expression in a few quick strokes.

I browsed the sketches. They were excellent, lifelike; they showed an ease that caused me a pang of envy. Each one captured the personality of the subject. Each one was professionally signed and dated. A few could probably be framed and sold. Not much money in it, but it was pretty clear Tamara was in dire straits. I set the best pieces aside.

Then I saw it.

It was a clean, beautiful sketch, a studio in chiaroscuro, a group scene, probably done as a warm-up number. I could visualize Damiano sitting in the dehors, the steaming cappuccino by his elbow, the pencil dancing in the cream-colored paper. A man and two young women, sitting at a round table, somewhere by the sea. They were relaxed, laughing. The man had a square jaw and thin mustache. He was smoking, and there was a darkness about him that made me shiver. One of the girls was playing with a strand of her hair.

I knew the two girls, the blonde and the redhead with the mole on her cheekbone.

I still dreamed about them.

They were both dead.

After dinner, I took a bicycle ride down to Santo Stefano. I still had the paper clippings in their folder, in one of the boxes beneath my berth. I recovered the stuff and took a long walk along the pier. I felt like I was on the edge of a deep, deep pit, waiting to jump in.

Next morning, over our usual coffee, I placed the sketch in front of Tamara.

"What's this?" she asked.

"Just take a good look at the drawing, please."

She shrugged and studied the pencil lines, holding the papers.

"Now look at these. The question is, are they the same girls?"

She squinted, stood and went by the window, scanning the photographs.

"They look like the same girls," she said finally.

"They look like, or they are the same?"

She snorted. She tilted her head on one side, and brought the photographs closer.

"They are the same," she said.

"Are you sure?"

"I'm positive. There's the beauty spot. And look at the ring..."

I stood by her side and squinted in turn. Danielle Ramin was wearing a big, vulgar ring on her right hand. The same ring graced the hand of the blonde on the promenade in Damiano's sketch.

I closed my eyes and took a long breath.

"What does this mean?" Tamara asked. "Is the thing worth something?"

I took another deep breath, the ghost of my aching ribs tickling my side. "I think so, yes. Quite a bundle, actually."

She asked something, probably if I could sell it, or what she could make out of it, but I was barely listening. "I need help on this one," I said.

In Santo Stefano, I found a photographer specializing in marriages and other ceremonies. I had photos of the sketch made, paying double to make it fast. Then I slipped two large prints in an envelope and mailed them to Jacques Granger.

I added a short note: 'Sanremo, September 1952. We've been had.'

I hit the Sanremo waterfront.

Tamara knew where her father plied his trade along the promenade. I started at one end of the marina and walked all the way to the city limits and then back. Twice. I stopped in bars, cafeterias, ice cream places, small bistros, restaurants and 'tavole calde'. I spoke to owners, cooks, cashiers, waiters. I went through the back of closed establishments, wading through stacked boxes of empty bottles, chatting up bartenders, waitresses, cooks having a smoke break. Some guys were friendly, other suspicious. One or two asked for my documents, one signaled he'd need a little help, by brushing together his thumb and fingertips. Ice cream parlors were the worst: a lot of them were closed, the owners back in Cuneo, Turin, Milan, running patisseries and bars in the off season. In three days I consumed a mountain of finger food, cold drinks, sandwiches. In a place called 'Eden', that was both a bar and a newsagent, I bought two chocolate pralines called 'boers'. There was a game, numbers inside the wrapping. I won a total of eight more. I stuffed them in my pocket, to save them for Tamara.

It took me three days to locate the place where the sketch had been done. It was in front of the 'Bagni La Brezza'.

With low grey clouds rolling in and the cold wind blowing, the beach had been closed, and the bar's the dehors had been dismantled. I sat inside, ordered a coffee. It was a slow day, a slow season, probably a slow year. A woman looking like a bored librarian sat in a corner, nursing a hot chocolate. On the radio, Claudio Villa followed the Quartetto Cetra, and then it was Yves Montand's turn. I sipped my coffee, took a good look around, and then picked an abandoned newspaper from a nearby table, and took a look at the front page. Good old Dwight Eisenhower was the new president of the US of A. I read the story, the numbers, the

hopes and misgivings. Finally, it was time to pay for my coffee, and I struck a conversation with the busty gal behind the cash register.

She remembered Damiano. She was seriously moved when I told her about the accident. We drank a peg to his memory.

"He was a nice man," she said. "Cheerful, very elegant."

There are worst epitaphs.

She remembered the two girls, too. "They were loud. Laughed a lot."

A bunch of tourists, they were, she said. "Big spenders. Regulars at the casino."

Did she know if they were they staying in some hotel, I asked.

She shook her head, and then patted her bottle blonde bouffant.

"Oh, no," she said. "They had a boat."

The letter arrived two days later. I was expecting a telegram, but I got an envelope through express courier.

The envelope contained a fat check, to cover for my 'expenses', a phone number, and a short note that basically said "find them, and leave the cops out of it."

Sure, leave the cops out.

What did he expect me to do?

It took me two weeks to find the 'Mermaid'.

Registered in Bastia, she was an old fishing boat converted to floating playground for a guy called Maurice Lassard, who chartered rich punters in the triangle of Mediterranean between the Cote d'Azur, the Tuscan Archipelago and the Corsican port of Bastia.

Of the five names I had on my list, it was the only one Granger had been able to place on the Provence coast at the time of the Ramin Affair. I sailed south, hoping to catch the boat in Elba, but when I got there the 'Mermaid' was gone already.

The Mediterranean was getting rough, Christmas was getting close, and the Elba port authority office looked like it had been ransacked and abandoned, a long time ago.

"The season's over, " the old harbor master told me as we shared some of his coffee and some of my cognac. "Lassard's probably back home."

"Bastia?" I asked. The Mermaid was registered there.

He shook his head, pouring some more cognac in his cup. "Or something."

I placed a photo of the Ramin girls in front of him.

He chuckled. "Big haul, eh?" he grinned.

"These two are still traveling with him?"

He nursed his spiked coffee and arched an eyebrow. "Why are you looking for him, again?"

"He owes me money," I said.

"Money, uh. So this has nothing to do with the chicks."

I shrugged. "I'm just checking." He gave me a look. "I'd hate him blowing my dough on some tramps."

"Not these. These are no mercenaries. They are the sort who hire, if you get my meaning, not hirelings themselves."

He looked out of his post's window, at the sea. It was choppy, the color of dishwater. "I guess he owes enough to justify the risk, what?"

"Quite a lot, yes."

I slipped him a ten thousand lire banknote, folded in four, Dante Alighieri eyeing me with suspicion from the pink, crispy paper.

The man laid his open palm on the money, and swept them in his pocket. "A small place up coast from Bastia," he finally said, rolling the empty glass in his fingers. "Saint something. The 'Mermaid' winters there, usually."

He pursed his lips, squinting. "The guy's bad news, you know that."

"I heard stories."

"Stories!" He laughed, and shook his head. "Likely they are true."

"I'll take my chances."

I had heard stories all right.

Maurice Lassard was a small-time hustler, thirty-something and not exactly the sharpest tool in the shed. He had started out as a sailor on freight ships before the war. Then, with the occupation, he had become very friendly with the Italians, and after the War had been chummy with Allied officers wishing to spend some time on the Riviera. Marseille, Nice, Monte Carlo, Menton, Ventimiglia. And Sanremo.

Probably some smuggling on the side. Cigarettes, penicillin, morphine, but always playing small. He was a third-tier hood.

He was tall, strong and good-looking. After the GIs had packed their stuff and left, he had moved his sights on nubile women. American, English, a few French and Italian young things. He knew the hot spots; he had the right friends. He had a boat, he was up for hire.

Square chin and a boxer's broken nose, Lassard also had

gained fame for his brutality - barroom brawls, but also the occasional job as hired muscle.

And now, he had landed himself two hot chicks and two million Francs.

And he had killed two women.

Why the hell was he still lingering in Europe?

PART THREE

I approached the harbor of Saint-Devote from the southeast, 'Le Corsair' riding on a chill wind over slate-colored waves.

Santa Devota, as the Italians called it, looked like a chunk of Morocco splattered on a flat stretch of Ligurian Sea coast. A fishermen's village, smack in front of Monaco, the iron-grey hills of Corsica at its back, Saint-Devote had it all: scenic harbor, good port, a cluster of low houses crowded around the old citadel. The Genoese had built it, and the place looked exotic and strange. Saint-Devote was a small place, less than one thousand people according to the tourist guide I had borrowed. Beautiful beaches, ancient church built by the Italians. It would have made an ideal spot for tourists, but there was no hotel, no accommodation to be had. Apparently the locals did not like strangers very much. And one could not really blame them: the Corsicans had been invaded, annexed or colonized by anyone, by the Greek and the Carthaginians, the Romans, Genoa and Pisa in the Renaissance, down to the Italians, the Nazis and the French in the twentieth century. With a track record like that, people might get a little wary of strangers.

The place was too small to have more than a jetty and an old automatic signal light, probably a leftover from the Italian occupation. The fishing boats were beached, their nets rolled up in ling gray snakes on the gravelly beach. The inlet was deep, the sea floor falling away a few dozen yards from the beach, small sloops, and a British two-master rocked slowly on their anchor chains. Closer to the headland rocks, the Mermaid sat in a nice place in the wind-shadow. It was a squat thing, its workhorse origins evident in its rough lines.

I dropped anchor about fifty yards from the Brits. A guy in an ascot cravat and an admiral cap waved a greeting, I waved back. The two-master was called 'Lady Daphne'.

I put some coffee on, pulled out and deployed a fishing tackle. Then I wrapped myself in a blanket, sat on the poop deck, and I started my stakeout.

Le Corsair is a 28-feet sloop. It was built between the wars, and it features a small kitchen, and even smaller bathroom. There's a table that can seat four if they are good friends, and if you're alone it might even feel spacious. The berths are none to write home about, but the poop deck is large enough for sun chair. Comfy, all things considered. So I spent three days like that, pretending to be a guy wasting his time and fishing, all the while studying the city, the coast road and the 'Mermaid' through my binoculars.

There were three men on the 'Mermaid', a skeleton crew working loose shifts. One man was always on the lookout, even at night. I spotted them as they lit their cigarettes up in the darkness.

Time slowed down as I sat there, eating my supplies, drinking coffee and sleeping in my short berth, my legs getting cramped, my eyes watery and my mood becoming darker. In three days, all the boats left the inlet apart from my prey and the British ship. Leaving two crewmen on board, the Admiral and his woman would land every afternoon. They usually came back between ten and eleven in the night.

Nothing moved, nothing happened.

Stretched out along the curve of the bay, Saint-Devote was white and still like a skeleton.

Now what?

If you want some apples, my grandfather used to say, you have got to give the tree a shake.

It was time to try and shake the tree.

As the sun set on the third day, I rowed on my tender to the beach of Saint-Devote. A guy was smoking on the poop deck of the 'Mermaid'. He looked at me as I passed him by. My collar turned up against the cold and my cap hiding my eyes, I nodded a greeting, and he replied by lifting a hand. I wondered if he was one of Pillowcase's band. In the growing dusk I was pretty sure he would not recognize me.

I landed and took some wood-legged steps, looking around. It was Friday night, and Saint-Devote looked dead. I walked up a crooked lane through whitewashed houses, and reached the main square, in front of the old church. Only a rusty phone booth by the side signaled the twentieth century had arrived even here. Three men sat on a bench in front of a wine joint, beneath the only streetlight in town. They stared at me like they wanted to x-ray me. They looked like the famous three monkeys, but it was pretty obvious they saw and heard everything, and would have no problem talking about it. Each of them held a walking cane in his hands, leaning over it. Caps, unshaven chins, black turtlenecks under faded jackets, they projected all the warmth and sympathy their people had probably given the Italians, and the Nazis, the Moorish raiders and the Florentine privateers, and probably the Carthaginians before them.

Welcome to Saint-Devote.

"Caught anything?"

The man in the apron placed a basket with olive bread on my table.

"Not enough," I replied.

He nodded, his hands hidden underneath his apron.

"If you're hungry, I can offer you a minestra, or baccala." He eyed me, sizing me up. "Or both."

I ordered the baccala, with a quart of white wine.

I broke a piece of the bread while I waited.

It was not a busy night in the old tavern. The two Brits were sitting at a table, enjoying a soup. The Admiral's woman was thin and cold, taking spoonfuls of minestra as if it was some bitter medicine. She exchanged a few words with the man. Not her husband. No ring, wrong body language.

Her face was finely chiseled. Long straight nose, high cheekbones, thin lips perpetually curled in a smile so cold it was no smile at all. She was elegant, poised and aristocratic. I wondered if maybe she was the celebrated Lady Daphne herself.

They made a show of not seeing me.

I dined, trying without any luck to involve mine host in something more than small talk. No biscuit. He was as taciturn as a wood Indian.

Nobody else came in the tavern through the evening.

It was like Saint-Devote was some kind of twilight place, like Brigadoon or something.

The Brits left, and the man in the apron cleared their table, glancing at me.

All of a sudden the idea of coming here alone felt very stupid.

But there was something, gnawing at the back of my head, and it was not Granger's request to keep the police out of the picture. I felt I owed it to the two young women in the burned Tube truck, whoever they had been, who had died in fire to cover for the two rich girls. I owed it to Madame Ramin, too, with her self-righteous steely blue stare and her repressed fury, and her desire to make the killers suffer. I could relate to that.

And then there was Damiano, guilty of sketching the wrong faces.

Knocked out, killed, abandoned along the road, in a ditch.

I wanted Lassard.

Lassard was only mine.

I wished good night to the man in the apron and nodded at his farewell grunt. Hostility with a chaser.

Saint-Devote was dark and lonely, silent as a funeral home and twice as cold. I pushed my hands in my pockets and walked back to the beach and my dingy, wondering if my brief night on the town would produce some change in the general stillness.

I did not have to wonder long.

There were two of them, discretely hanging in the shadow of a fishing boat, invisible in the on/off light of the automatic signal light.

Had it not been for the chill wind.

"My ass is freezing!"

"Shut up you moron!"

They were staking my rowboat.

I crouched, observing the scene as the light from the jetty swept over the beach. Were there more of them?

Minutes ticked by.

"Where the hell is he?"

The other shushed him, a nasty hiss.

Then the one who had spoken first moved, gravel creaking under his feet. He took two steps, wrapping his arms around himself. His pal's call hissed call "Henri!" did not stop him.

"I say he won't show up," Henri said.

The other man was big, heavy. He grabbed his companion by the lapel of his jacket and dragged him back. "His boat's here," he said, in a low gravelly voice. "He will come."

The other shrugged.

More steps on the gravel, this time on my left.

The two men retreated in the shadows.

The Admiral and his thin woman came walking arm in arm, talking softly.

They got to their dinghy, and as she waited, arms crossed, one foot tapping, he laughed out loud and started pushing the boat in the water.

My ticket home.

I moved. "Let me help!"

Lady Daphne jumped and looked at me, squinting, while the Admiral turned and stared.

I walked swiftly to them. "May I help you?" I repeated, as cheerfully as possible. "You know, neighborly courtesy."

The admiral smiled, broadly. "You the chap from the sloop? Le Corsair?"

Too loud, too cheerful. I felt steps behind me. I was such a fool.

I raised my hands as the Admiral pulled out a small compact gun.

A fist slammed in my face.

Surprised, I staggered and took two steps back.

"Not in the face, you moron!" the big one said.

Henri grabbed me by the lapels. I rammed a knee in his crotch and pushed him back. He gurgled, took a tentative step and fell to his knees.

The other planted his hand between my shoulders and pushed me forward.

"Enough of these games!" said the Admiral, waving his gun about.

Henri stood, breathing heavily.

The signal light flashed in his eyes as he hit me again.

The big man held me up, then he walked around me. He grabbed my wrists and tied them.

The English woman was staring at me, her arms crossed, the collar of her fine windcheater up against the cold. Her face was a pale oval. She kept tapping her feet impatiently.

The big man tightened the knots on my wrists. "Now we gonna go for a little boat ride, eh, mon ami?"

Henri hit me again, this time in the gut.

Then they dragged me to my rowboat.

"We'll make it look like a boating accident," the big man said. He pulled a length of rope from his pocket and tied my ankles, while his pal rowed us offshore. "You drank too much, the boat capsized, you drowned." A shrug. "Happens all the time."

I lifted my hands. "With my arms and legs tied?"

The big man shrugged again, and shook his head. "Happens all the time," he repeated.

"I knew you're full of shit, Canard!" Henri growled, heaving on the oars. "I should have roughed him up a little more."

"Waste of time."

"He kicked my balls!"

The Canard laughed. "Proves you've got them, eh, Henri?"

The other glowered but was silent.

The Brits followed us, their small outboard engine thrumming softly. The signal light kept blinking, turning the low mist into a ghostly, pearlescent layer hanging over the black water.

"We're far enough," Henri said, finally.

"Keep going."

When the Canard reckoned we were far enough from the shore, he pulled out a gun, holding it level at my chest. He motioned for me to stand with the barrel of his gun. "Jump," he said.

I stared at him, trying not to look too surprised or too happy.

"Just like that?" I asked, taking a big lungful of air.

With a grunt, Henri kicked me overboard.

When you hit the ice-cold water, the first automatic reaction is to open your mouth and take a long breath. Bad thinking, because it's not sweet air that you breathe in. So you have to make an effort not to take a big gulp. That's the first thing, if you want to survive.

Then you have to ignore the cold, which bites your extremities, making you so numb you can't feel your face anymore. In the cold water, your heart starts pumping faster, and the air in your lungs pushes to break through your lips. You must remember this is supposed to happen anyway, and keep your wits about you.

I sank slowly, the intermittent light from the jetty becoming fainter and farther away. I kicked my shoes off, then attacked the rope around my wrists with my teeth. The morons should have tied my hands at my back. It would have made the thing a lot trickier. This way, in twenty seconds straight I had loosened the knot enough to free my hands.

An icy spike pushing through my chest, I swam with

all my energy.

Reactivate the circulation, get the energy flowing, and get as far as possible from the point where I'd been dumped.

Ten, fifteen, thirty heartbeats, swimming in the utter blackness. Then I pushed up and surfaced as quietly as possible. I heard voices in the distance, accompanied by the beat of the outboard engine.

I was suspended between water and mist, the air around me shimmering white every five heartbeats. Somewhere the dinghy's outboard putt-putting rose in gear as the Brits went back to their two-master.

Shivering, I bent double and freed my ankles.

When I resurfaced, I tried to get my bearings. The cold was making it hard to think. The few lights of the coast were dim and distant, a handful of fireflies a million miles away.

Keeping the jetty light at my back, I started swimming, a slow but steady, disciplined crawl. I stopped every fifty strokes to check my position, and scan the short horizon, a hazy line between black sea and milky fog.

On my fourth stop, something swam by my feet, cold in the colder water, inspecting this strange intruder in its habitat. I ignored it and kept going. Breathing became harder, cramps slashed through my calves and thighs. Fifty strokes and then a stop. Then another fifty. And again.

Then the chill breeze died. I was in the shadow of the headland: the fog was thicker, the air was still, and the position lights of Le Corsair were blinking welcome to me.

I kept swimming with arms and legs made of stone. The cold water was turning me into a statue, I thought. I would sink and lie on the bottom of the bay, like some ancient Roman artifact, for future archaeologists to find me. Then my hands grabbed the anchor chain.

Relief was such that I was tempted to hang there for a few minutes, collecting my energies. I forced myself to hold tighter to the chain, and painfully, slowly, I hauled myself up.

In the darkness of the Le Corsair's hold, I got rid of my

soaked clothes and wrapped myself in a thick blanket. Shivers were so bad it took me three matches to light up the stove under the water boiler. Teeth chattering, I sat by the small table and rubbed my arms through the blanket, trying to restart the blood circulation.

When the worst of the shakes was over, I recovered a brandy bottle from the closet underneath my seat, together with a tin cup and the box of black tea. I put the stuff on the table and poured myself half a cup of brandy. I drank it slowly, cherishing the warmth spreading through my chest.

Diesel motors coughed in the dark. Through a porthole, I saw the Lady Daphne maneuver slowly to leave the bay. The Brits were leaving in haste. I poured myself a second brandy.

Outside, something splashed in the water, then thumped against the hull of my ship.

I had visitors.

"I can't see why we can't wait till tomorrow," a familiar voice was complaining. Boots thumped on the deck.

A grunt. "We wanna be un-con-spicuous," the Canard said, mockingly. They both laughed. "That British bastard."

"Lassard will be pissed all right," Henri remarked.

"I think their business was done, anyway," replied the other. "And it's our asses that are freezing anyway, eh?"

The Canard laughed. "You'd love to be up there in his place, eh?"

With a mumbled curse, Henri lit a torchlight and peered through the hatchway. I threw the boiling water in his face.

He screamed, and retreated, covering his face with his hands.

He let drop the torch. Taking two steps backwards, he stumbled on his partner.

I sprang through the hatch, brandishing the water boiler like a bludgeon. I hit the blinded man in the head, pushed him by the side, reached his pal and slammed the dented metal pot in his face, once, twice.

Henri tumbled over the side and fell overboard, the splash smothering his wail. I was alone with the big one. The on-off light from the jetty shone on the Canard's rage-contorted features, his bleeding nose. He growled and reached for me, arms outstretched. I ducked, tried to kick him in a knee but we were too close to each other.

From the water came the furious splashes of Henri.

The Canard sidestepped, putting himself in a corner. I hit his crotch with the ball of my foot. He threw his head back, gurgling. Still gripping my impromptu weapon in my right, I rabbit-punched him in the throat with a fast left. He chocked, trapped against the railing, and spent two seconds too many to decide his next move. I was cold, tired and furious. I crashed the water boiler against his temple, with a hollow, discordant chiming sound, and his lights went out.

Naked in the mist, shivering, I looked over the side. The other guy was trying to reach for the side rail, his hands slapping the side of the hull. His head bobbed over the dark surface for a few seconds, then his blind eyes widened and he simply sank out of view. Soon the sea was again black and undisturbed.

I recovered a rope and a grease-stained piece of rag from the box beneath the wheel. As fast as I could, I tied the big man's wrists behind his back, and then tied them again to his ankles. I found his gun and threw it overboard. Then I pushed the rag in his mouth, and finally retreated to the warmth of my cabin.

I only needed an address, and the Canard revealed it through chattering teeth, a thin layer of rime reflecting the dawn's early light, looking like a sugar frosting over his clothes, skin and hair.

I pushed the rag back and with a heave I dumped him in the dingy. Rowing to the coast helped me warm up. The Canard kept looking at me with bovine eyes.

"Afraid I'll do you the same service you did to me, are you?"

He chewed on his gag.

"Well, I won't."

More chewing and mumbling.

"Believe me if I say I'm sorry for poor Henri," I told him.

I jumped ashore and pulled my boat high and dry on the gravelly beach. "You wait here, OK?"

He moaned. I pulled a tarpaulin over the boat, then walked up to the main square. Too early for there being anyone in sight. I entered the phone booth on the corner of the square, and made two calls.

The first to Granger, the second to the cops in Bastia.

The house was high on the cliffs overlooking Saint-Devote.

It was a gentrified box of stone. Whitewashed walls of uneven rocks and mortar, six windows facing the sea, two on the ground floor, four on the top floor. A wide terrace with cold-burned potted plants, a small courtyard with an old US Army-issue olive-green Jeep parked in the front. On the south side, a glass winter garden had been built, in an attempt at gentrification. Long neglected, it was filled with plants run amok, the iron skeleton of the glasshouse red with rust.

Twin wisps of smoke escaped through the two chimneys and faded into the gray sky. The place was uncannily silent.

I jumped the wall.

No glass shards on top, no guard dogs, no sentries.

I took a tour of the grounds. An abandoned shed, an overgrown lawn.

In the shed, an assortment of rusty garden tools, half a bag of weeds killer, a water line, coiled like a sleeping snake. A metal box with some clutches and screwdrivers, and a small rusty saw.

Looking at the house from the shadow of the shed, through a small window I saw Danielle Ramin, blonde hair a halo around her impish face. She was wrapped in a thick dressing gown, and she struggled with some eggs in a skillet. As I watched her, Maurice Lassard entered the kitchen. He was smoking a cigarette. He circled Danielle's waist from behind, pulling her against his chest.

She laughed as he slipped a hand inside her gown, weighing

her breast. She laughed and squealed. In response he took his hand out and stretched it over the stove, as if to warm it.

Coquettish, she gestured with her spoon towards the table, and he walked to his seat, lingering a moment to squeeze her bottom.

A real charmer, monsieur Lassard.

I checked the time. Ten past seven.

Fiery-headed Valerie rushed in the kitchen. She was dressed in slacks and a blouse. "They're gone!" she shouted, staring daggers at Lassard.

"What?!"

The trio ran out of the kitchen.

Time to get to work. Yesterday I had shaken the tree, now it was time to cut it down.

Cracking a lock with a screwdriver is not hard. It's not subtle, either, but I was not interested in subtlety. I needed speed.

I walked into the kitchen. The smell of food was strong. I picked a piece of crispy bacon on the way. Lassard and the two Ramin girls where out in the front. They were very excited. "They're gone!" Valerie was repeating. I imagined them scanning the bay, searching for the 'Lady Daphne', maybe passing a pair of binoculars between them.

I tiptoed upstairs. The stairs creaked. I stopped, listened, started up again. A landing, three doors.

Question: you have three million Francs in cash.

What do you do?

Do you stash the duffel bag under your bed?

In truth, I would have expected something like that from Lassard. But judging from the racket downstairs, and by the way she was verbally thrashing the poor man, I was beginning to believe Valerie Ramin was the brain of the outfit. And Valerie was, if not smarter, at least more sophisticated than her sister's boyfriend.

As Granger had said, they were sitting on the sort of money

that has its own gravitational pull. No use having such money and not putting it to work. But to put money to work, you need banks. And banks don't like huge amounts of questionable cash.

I checked the first room.

Lassard's lair was littered with empty bottles. A huge unmade bed, the covers piled at the foot, and spilling on the floor. There was a 1911A resting on the bed stand. I pulled out the magazine, put it in my pocket, and with my left thumb I pushed out the bullets as I walked around. Clothes strewn about, a big Louis Whatever chair covered in discarded shirts and rumpled trousers. I threw the stuff on the floor. The chair looked authentic. A chest filled with more clothes. I checked the wardrobe. Jackets, a windcheater, an overcoat. Cash in a jacket pocket. A few thousands in a gold money clip. I pocketed them and went on checking. More small change in other pockets. A switchblade. I slipped that in my pocket too.

Downstairs, the discussion had moved indoors and it had heated, but apart from the tones, it was impossible to understand what the guys were saying. Valerie was doing much of the talking.

I slipped the empty magazine back in the Colt and I moved to the next door. A smaller room, window open facing south, letting in the early morning sun. A big bed with a thick mattress, a mess of sheets and blankets, thick pillows. A wardrobe. I checked it.

Two fine dresses, a stack of denim pants, blouses, jackets. Sensible shoes. Valerie's room.

I patted the jackets.

Bingo.

In the inside pocket, a leather wallet. Seven checks, from the cashiers of the casinos of Monaco and Sanremo. Lots of money, in French Francs and Italian Lire. I made a quick mental calculation. About three hundred grand and change.

So, here's your answer: you launder the cash and turn it into something banks actually like. And if you are on the Cote d'Azur, that's pretty straightforward.

It goes like this.

You take a small amount of your stash, put on your best

duds, and take a night out on the town, paying a visit to the local casino. There's two of them on the coast, one in Monaco, the other in Italy, in Sanremo. The places are about one seventy miles apart, so you can play both. You get in the casino and you change some money. Let's say you buy fiches for one hundred thousand Francs, cash. You find yourself a table or roulette, you sit down and bet five thousand on the red. Or on the black, it doesn't matter. Both have a fifty/fifty chance of turning up and pay one to one, so unless you're really jinxed, you'll suffer a minimal erosion of your finances. All you have to do is sit there and play your five thousand, again and again. A little winning, a little losing, and in the end you'11 have the same money you started
with, give or take five thousand. You can play for about one hour, one hour and a half. At this point, you stand, leave a tip 'pour les emploies', and go cash in your 'wins', as a handy, totally legit, state-guaranteed, squeaky clean check. Exactly the sort of money banks love.

Nice and smooth.

I kept searching. Inside a small snappy handbag I found another wallet, this one in bright green crocodile hide, holding another bunch of checks. Another one hundred and fifty.

Voices came upstairs. Trampling feet.

The door opened, and Valerie Ramin stood there, her sister flush behind her. Valerie stared at me, mouth open.

"Your mom sends her best wishes," I said.

She jumped at me with an animal screech. Her thin body slammed in my chest, and I took a step back, stumbled, and we both fell on her big bed. Our weight burst one of her thick feather pillows. White feathers erupted around us. She punched me in the face, then tried to scratch my eyes out. I spit a feather out, then pushed Valerie off. She grabbed my arms and we were like that, me on my back and she sitting astride of me, when Lassard pushed Danielle out of his way and pointed his Colt at us.

"It's not like you think!" I said.

He cocked his gun.

Valerie and I rolled off the bed. We stood, and I pulled her over and used her as a shield. She smelt of sweat and expensive soap. She tried to break my hold. "Let me go, you bastard!"

I held her closer, my hand gripping her arm, and eyed Lassard.

"Didn't I kill you already?" he said.

I chuckled. "Scared about ghosts?"

He kept the gun pointed at us. "You're not a ghost, you're a coward."

"Said the one with a gun..."

"You won't get out of here alive, coward."

I felt Valerie's blood racing, her heart pounding against my chest.

"I won't go alone," I said.

She stiffened. Her sister was kneeling on the floor by the door, staring at the scene.

Lassard glanced at her. "Remember what you said, honey?" he said.

Danielle's eyes widened. "Wh...what?"

"You always wanted to be the only child, right?"

Danielle screamed as Lassard pulled the trigger.

Click.

In the feather-filled room, silence crashed like a thunder.

"Bad choice of friends, babe," I whispered in Valerie's ear.

I pushed her on the bed, turned and jumped through the window.

I rolled on the glass roof of the greenhouse and tried to get back on my feet. Before I could get my bearings, Lassard crashed into me, growling.

Our weight was too much for the tired structure. Iron rafters bent and glass exploded, and we fell through into the withered jungle beneath, in a shower of shards. A thick mattress of brown leaves cushioned our fall, and we tumbled in a jumble of snapped branches, dead leaves and broken pottery.

I stood. Lassard kicked me in the side, and I rolled on the cluttered floor, my ribs screaming, winded.

I turned, pushing with my back against the glass wall to stand up. Standing in front of me, Lassard had a big terracotta vase in his hands and took a step forward, aiming at my head. I rushed at him, grabbing him by the waist, carrying him along with my momentum. The vase escaped his hands and exploded on the tiled floor. Screaming an obscenity, Lassard punched me on the side. Breath escaped painfully from my lungs and I let him go. I slipped; he clutched my wrist and pulled me forward. I hit him in the face with my left, straightened, and kicked him in a knee. We fell again in the thick of the dead plants. His arm locked around my neck.

"Die!" he roared in my ear.

His left punched me again in the ribs, his right elbow pressing on my carotid like a vice. I saw black dots floating in the air. My heart beat like a bell in the depths of the ocean. I thought I heard a distant thunder, rolling in the hills above the old house.

I put my hand in my pocket. I flicked the knife, and stabbed Lassard in his thigh. I pushed the blade in deep, then twisted.

He screamed and let me go.

I fell on all fours, coughing.

I looked up.

Valerie Ramin was standing in the door of the greenhouse, Lassard's Colt in her hand. She stared at me in the eye. Her eyes were green, pale, and dead. "Shoot, love!" Lassard barked.

And she blew his head off.

There was a siren, wailing up the road.

Valerie would not let go of the gun. I pushed her hand down, and then pressed hard on her wrist. The gun clattered on the floor. The redhead found a big wicker chair and sat heavily in it. She was pale and disheveled.

Time to vacate the premises.

Through the door, I was back in the entrance hall. Halfway

up the staircase, Danielle Ramin was laying on her back where she had fallen. Her blood trickled down the steps. Her eyes open, her face frozen in an expression of surprise.

I went through the kitchen and out the back door.

The cops were kicking down the front door as I jumped the garden wall.

Another gunshot echoed from the house.

By the time I was back on the beach, I was looking somewhat civilized again. The three men on the square were discussing with two women in black about the police cars they had seen go up the hillside.

I pulled the tarpaulin away.

Le Canard laid there, his wrists tied to his ankles. He did not move when I undid the knots and slowly rolled the rope up. He eyed me with his big bovine eyes, munching on the dirty rag.

I pulled the rag out, grasped him by the lapels and bodily dragged him out of my boat. "Get the hell away."

My voice croaked. I felt one hundred years old. There had been enough dead in this ugly story. He just stared at me.

"Get the fuck out," I shouted, "before I change my mind!"

He took one tentative step, keeping his eyes on me, then another. Then he started running.

I watched him run into Saint-Devote and disappear, as I rowed back to Le Corsair.

I was passing by the 'Mermaid' as one of the crew came out, rubbing his arms in the cold, and then stretched with a yawn. He waved hallo, I saluted him back.

He was staring at the high house on the cliff, shielding his eyes with a hand against the sun, as I docked with Le Corsair.

Half an hour later Saint-Devote was behind me.

In the end, Valerie did not manage to blow her brains out.

She just caused a bad burn on her temple, and a scar, and much drama and consternation. I half expected the newspapers to be all over the affair, but there was little more than half a column on page twenty-one. The cops did not make much sense of the whole business, but they did patch together a story that sounded vaguely convincing. Kidnapping. Simulated deaths. White slave market. Whatever. Then the girls had tried to escape, possibly with the help of a gang member that was nowhere to be found.

Lassard had shot Danielle, and Valerie had shot Lassard.

She was badly shocked.

She was being sent back home.

All's well that ends well.

Or something.

EPILOGUE

Granger puffed on his Montecristo as I helped myself to a second serving of the saffron and bacon spaghetti. I hate it when people smoke at the table, but it was his treat, his choice of restaurant, I couldn't really complain.

"Did you get any lead on the Lady Daphne?" I asked.

He made a face, pursing his lips, rolling his eyes in my direction.

"I don't think you should waste your time pursuing that ship," he said. "Or its passengers."

I swallowed a mouthful. "They were Lassard's accomplices," I said. But the role of the Brits was still a matter of debate.

Had they been Lassard's helpers in the money laundering?

People connected with some other shady deal of him?

Granger waved his hand. "More or less, yes."

He took a long drag from his cigar and leaned back in his chair. "But I sincerely hope you will let those sleeping dogs lay, as the saying goes."

I studied his face. He was not joking. "What do you know about those people?"

"More than I'd wish to, my friend," he said, "And enough for me to suggest you let them go."

I drank some water. "The Mediterranean is not that big."

"If they have any sense, they are well out of the Med already."

"They'll be back," I said. "And I'll be here."

"Please, don't."

A dapper waiter came and cleared our plates. "May I serve le loup de mer?" he asked softly.

Granger gestured for him to go on. Then he slipped a hand in his jacket and pulled out a fat envelope. "Madame Ramin sends her regards," he said.

I eyed the yellow envelope. "I doubt she's very grateful about the way I handled the whole affair."

Granger stared at the tip of his cigar. "You don't know her."

He pushed the envelope closer to me. "Old military family, duty before affection, that sort of thing. The red-headed bitch will regret she's not in the slammer."

"Even if she's the Joan of Arc of the whole piece?" I asked.

Madame Ramin had been fed a nice little story. Maybe she did not believe it, but so far Granger, Valerie and I were the only ones that really knew what sort of Elizabethan tragedy this whole business had been. He did not reply, and just puffed on his cigar.

I picked the envelope and opened it. I ran my thumb on the wad of banknotes.

"Thirty grand," Granger said. "Looks like you're set, my boy."

"Did you count them?"

"You bet I did, they come from my funds."

I made a face at him. "Personal favor to the family, you know," he said.

I closed the envelope. "You keep them," I said.

A speechless Granger was no ordinary sight.

"I keep them?" he finally said, caressing the envelope.

"Yes. You've got friends in the Gendarmerie, right?"

He spread his hands, as if to say that of course he had.

"So here's the deal. You shake your contacts, and get the names of the two girls in that truck, that night."

He sighed. "I think I can see where this is going."

It was my turn to shrug. "As soon as you have the names, each family gets fifteen." I stared him in the eye. "Not a cent less."

He snorted, pretending amusement. "Do I have to attach a card to this liberality of yours?"

"Let's say they are from an anonymous benefactor."

The waiter arrived with the baked sea bass, and spent the following five minutes partitioning it and serving it to us. When he was finished. Granger put the envelope back in his pocket. "I will do as you request," he said.

The bass was excellent. "Fine," I said. "So this leaves only the small question of the seventy-five grand you owe me."

He chocked. "What?!"

People at nearby tables turned to us. I grinned at them.

"Finder's fee?" I said. "Ten percent's the rule, right?"

The fat man was outraged. "Finder's fee?" he repeated, his voice low. "Finder's...? It was you who lost them in the first place!"

"But I recovered them. Well, most of them."

He munched angrily on a chunk of white fish.

"You can't appreciate the taste and the texture, if you eat so fast," I said.

He cleaned his lips with his napkin. "You are crazy!"

The other customers still glancing at us, we ate in silence for a few minutes.

"Five thousand," he finally said, without lifting his gaze from his dish.

"You gotta be kidding. I was almost killed three times..."

"Exactly, almost."

"Fifty thousand."

He huffed, pouring himself a glass of wine. "Preposterous. Ten thousand."

"Fifteen."

"And no strings attached?"

I nodded. "None whatsoever."

"Deal."

We clicked glasses.

I pulled out pen and paper and I scratched down Tamara's address. "Here, have them delivered here."

He stared at the paper for fifteen seconds, then he burst out laughing. "You are still the same, aren't you?" he asked. "Still trying to save the world and all that stuff."

I wondered if the spark in his eyes was admiration or pity. I shrugged, and finished my fish.

Granger was still shaking his head. "These are for old man Bricco's daughter, eh?"

I nodded.

"Bad story," he said, pocketing my note. "He was so good. The Miser. A real artist. You ever saw the copy of the Manet he did for me, back in '34?"

I shook my head.

"Ah!" He sighed, putting down his fork. "Wrong place, wrong time, what? I'll see the girl gets them as soon as possible. Might even throw in another five thousand for old times' sake."

I leaned back. "Always a gentleman."

"We're a dying breed, my boy, mark my words. A dying breed." And then, "What about you?" he asked. "What do you get out of all this?"

I took my time drinking a glass of water. I had Lassard's cash and his gold clip, of course. And his antique chair. Even without a certified provenance, it had made me a nice wad of cash, well worth the bother of getting back in Saint-Devote, and breaking the police seals to retrieve it. But I thought all this was none of Granger's business. "I got Lassard," I shrugged, "and the two Ramin girls, in a way. And I'll get the 'Lady Daphne', sooner or later."

"Revenge is stupid, Leo. It does not pay for expenses."

I crossed my arms. "Let's not call it revenge, then. Let's call it just desserts."

The waiter was hovering by our side. "Monsieurs, desserts?"

I chuckled while Granger ordered a crème brûlée.

The End

Author's Afterword - On the Border

The fishing boats go out across the evening water
Smuggling guns and arms across the Spanish border
The wind whips up the waves so loud
The ghost moon sails among the clouds
Turns the rifles into silver on the border

(Al Stewart, On the Border)

I am pretty sure Al Stewart's song was playing in the back of my mind in March 2013 when, according to my notes, I jotted down the first ideas for something I thought I'd call The Corsair.

I'd just finished a brief chat with two friends – a chat about pulp stories, and pulp stories not set in the United States in particular.

I had pointed out that the Mediterranean, back in the '30s and '40s (the golden age of pulp), would be a perfect setting for character-driven fiction.

"Just think about the huge number of great stories set in the area," I said. "From For Whom the Bell Tolls to Mask of Dimitrios via To Catch a Thief and The Zoo Gang."

My plan was to do a series of stories, following the old "Lester Dent formula" and set between the World Wars. I'd market them as self-produced e-books, setting up the usual corollary of website, mailing list, extras, gadgets and whatnot. I would tell the story of an adventurer called Leo Martin – a name without a nationality, which sounds right in Italian, French, Spanish, English – as he sailed around the Mediterranean, facing mysteries, conspiracies, crime lords, Nazis and Fascists, spies and so forth. I even planned a recipe collection – because I saw my hero as a kind of bon vivant. It would be great. What could possibly go wrong?

I started reading to get my history straight, and started jotting down ideas.

But the thing went nowhere.

What I think really got in the way was the sense of gloom I got from reading history books about the Mediterranean area before the Second World War. Yes, the '30s were the age of style, but it was hard to think in terms of high, light-hearted adventure as dictators rose to power, poverty struck millions, and war and mass murder loomed closer.

I shelved the project – even if that image of gunrunners on the border kept returning.

"One of these days..." I thought.

It took me eighteen months to work out a solution. Other songs were probably playing in my mind as I decided to try and move the action forward in time, about two decades: Leo Martin landed in the 1950s, and soon every piece fell into place.

The 1950s still allowed ample space for adventure and derring-do, but the cheerfulness and the sunny sense of relief of the post-war years counterpointed nicely the darker forces still at work in the shadows of the economic bubble, of la Dolce Vita.

I realized that what I really wanted to write was not a Lester Dent-style hero pulp, but something closer to the works of David Dodge and Leslie Charteris, something moving along the same lines of "The Persuaders", a TV show I enjoyed as a kid. With plenty of thrills and adventure, a drop of noir, and a little humor, I wanted my hero to be savvy like Travis McGee and suave as TV's Lovejoy. I wanted him to chat with the reader, outwit the bad guys, pull the beautiful ladies, and maybe make a buck while he was at it. And the 1950s were just right. So I started with a party, on the French Riviera...

Now I don't want to pretend it was all downhill from there, one of those "And the story just wrote itself!" things of which some of my colleagues seem to be so fond; the first Le Corsaire story met its fair share of problems, dry spells, detours and rewrites. Real life hit hard while I was writing, but in the end it was all right.

I had to roam around the Mediterranean a lot, scouting for locations on Google Maps. In a fit of frustration, I moved the middle of the story from the Versilia coast of Tuscany to the Italian Riviera. And when history got in the way, I had to scrap my Corsican location, and invent a Corsican town from scratch (the only bit of complete geographical invention in this story).

Two or three characters were dropped, one was drowned and Tamara... ah, Tamara was originally called Marina - until I noticed that Marina's father painted marinas on the marina of Diano Marina, and I felt incredibly stupid.

But in the end, "Chasing the Mermaid" landed on the desk of my publisher - and he liked it, just as my beta readers had liked it. I know some pretty strange people.

They all helped a lot, so now the moment has come to thank them.

My gratitude goes to, in no particular order, Clara Giuliani, Marina Belli, Valentina Coscia, Lucia Patrizi and Marco Siena, Angelo Benuzzi and Germano "Hell" Greco, for their friendship, suggestions, enthusiasm and for helping me with my copy-blindness.

My brother Alessandro offered technical support and helped me try a few fight scenes – thanks, brother!

And of course a big thank you to Michael Hudson, for believing Le Corsaire was seaworthy.

And finally thank you to all my readers: if there are more stories coming, it's all thanks to you.

Be careful out there.

Davide Mana
Asti, Italy
Winter 2016

Davide Mana was born in Turin, Italy, 1967, and lives in Castelnuovo Belbo, a 900-souls community in the hills of the Monferrato area of Northern Italy. He studied science in Turin, Bonn, Urbino, receiving a BSc in Geology, and he's currently working on his PhD.

Davide has been a call center operator, language teacher, scarecrow, university researcher, freelance researcher, post-doc course teacher, translator, author, content crafter, art show coordinator, editor, lecturer, game designer, fantasy writer, teacher of Taoist Philosophy, book reviewer, web designer, and bicycle repairman.

An author of both fiction and non-fiction, he blogs both in Italian and English.

In his spare time he listens to music, plays at tabletop roleplaying games, cooks and watches old movies.

He's currently waiting for the dealer to deal him the next hand of cards.

RAVEN'S HEAD PRESS

Ramona Stewart's

DESERT TOWN

A HOTHOUSE MELODRAMA

DESERT TOWN is dark crime fiction for those who have a taste for the perverse and violent. It was made into a major film, DESERT FURY, starring Burt Lancaster, Lizabeth Scott and Mary Astor.

It's the story of seventeen year old Paula Haller as she transitions into womanhood while defying her mother, Fritzi's dominance. Fritzi runs the small town of Chuckawalla including the Purple Sage casino and saloon as well as a bordello or two. Fritzi can control everything but Paula and the tension between the two is drawn as tight as a drum.

The scenery includes sprawling ranches, a very much out of place colonial mansion and the beauty of the vast desert.

Mix in a notorious gangster, his insanely jealous business associate, a love triangle, some sadistic cops, weirdly eccentric characters and sexual innuendo aplenty.

Once the sun brings all these ingredients to a boil you've got the recipe for a crackerjack noir story like no other.

DOUBLE LANGUAGE
ONE
SHOT
ENGLISH :: ITALIANO

GIANLUCA PIREDDA

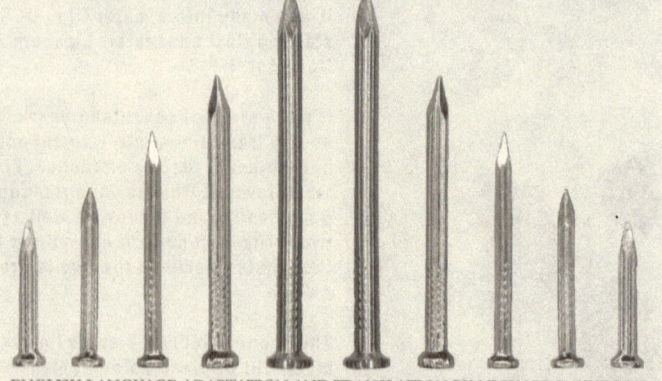

ENGLISH LANGUAGE ADAPTATION AND TRANSLATION BY MICHAEL R. HUDSON

WICKED GAME

A PSYCHOLOGICAL THRILLER

The Order of
THE DRAGON
An Amun Galeas and Sebastian Vulk Adventure
PHIL HORE

RAVEN'S HEAD PRESS edition $15.95 US • Order your copy
today from Amazon.com or ravensheadpress.com